MONA the VAMPIRE

The Jackpot Disaster

CINAR

Television series © 1999 Fancy Cape Productions Inc.
a subsidiary of CINAR Corporation/Alphanim, France
3, Canal J. All rights reserved.

ORCHARD BOOKS
96 Leonard Street, London EC2A 4XD
Orchard Books Australia
14 Mars Road, Lane Cove, NSW 2066
First published in Great Britain in 1996
This edition published in 2000
ISBN 1-84121-857-X
Text © Hiawyn Oram
Illustrations © Sonia Holleyman
The right of Hiawyn Oram to be identified as the
Author and Sonia Holleyman as the Illustrator of this
Work has been asserted by them in accordance with
the Copyright, Designs and Patents Act, 1988.
A CIP catalogue record for this book is available from
the British Library.
1 3 5 7 9 10 8 6 4 2
Printed in the United Kingdom

MONA the VAMPIRE

The Jackpot Disaster

Hiawyn Oram

Illustrated by
Sonia Holleyman

ORCHARD BOOKS

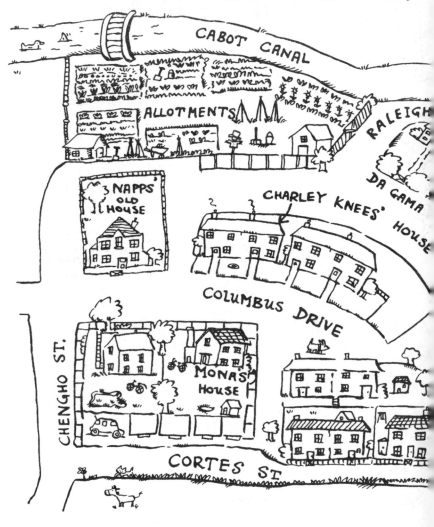

COLUMBUS CLOSE OFF OLD STREET

CABOT CANAL

ALLOTMENTS

RALEIGH

DA GAMA

NAPPS' OLD HOUSE

CHARLEY KNEES' HOUSE

COLUMBUS DRIVE

CHENGHO ST.

MONA'S HOUSE

CORTES ST.

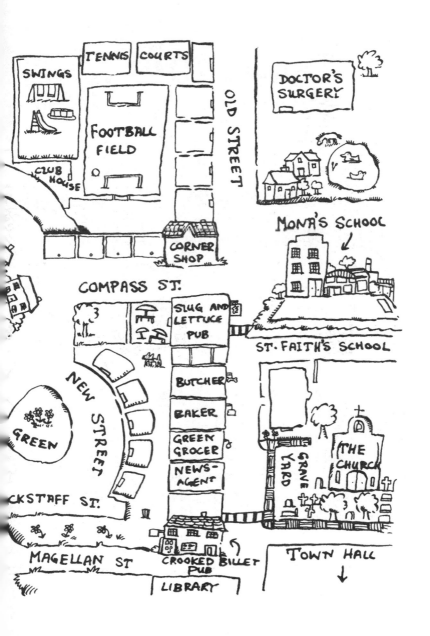

Contents

The Cast

Mona

Fang

Mum

Dad

Miss Gotto

Reverend Gregory

Chapter 1
Angela Turns Horrible

Angela was Mona and Fang's best friend. She was always over at Mona's or they were over at Angela's playing wonderful games. Their favourite was *Wild Ones*.

In *Wild Ones* they were two little girls and a human cat living in the forest with their wild ponies, Starlight and Bramble.

And it was in the middle of one of these games — just as they'd raced away from some wicked horse thieves — that Angela broke the news.

"My father's hit the jackpot," she announced in a strange high voice, "and we're moving to a new house. A huge house, a ginormous house with a ginormous swimming pool so I won't be able to be your best friend anymore. And I'll be getting a real pony so I won't have to play this silly make-believe game with you anymore, either."

Mona and Fang slunk home, devastated. They sat about at the kitchen table, devastated. Mona's father did his best funny alien to try and cheer them up. But Mona wouldn't be cheered up. She was choking back tears.

"What does hitting the jackpot mean?" she asked, miserable.

"Why?" said her father.

"Because Angela's dad has and it's made her really horrible and she doesn't want to play with us anymore ..." And now Mona couldn't hold back the tears. She bawled long and loud while Fang caterwauled.

"Oh dear, oh dear, oh dear!" said Mona's father, gathering Mona up. "Now, now ... there, there," he said.

"Comfort Fang too," sobbed Mona.

So Mona's father took Mona *and* Fang

in his arms and did his best to explain.

"These things happen in life. People hit jackpots and they change. Sometimes they change for the better and sometimes for the worse. If Angela has changed for the worse then you have to feel sorry for her. Just imagine how awful it must be to turn *so* horrible overnight ..."

But Mona couldn't imagine it. No matter how many jackpots her father

hit, she couldn't imagine not wanting to play *Wild Ones* with Fang and her best friend.

She didn't feel sorry for Angela either. She felt hurt and in terrible danger of Angela getting more horrible or even more and more horrible.

And so, the next morning, she completely insisted she go to school in her vampire things – as protection.

Special protecting Vampire Kit

Chapter 2
Angela the More Horrible v. the Vampire

It was good thinking. For a start, when Angela arrived at school in a huge white car and Charley-Knees went, "Wow! What a car!" and Angela went, "Well don't think you'll ever ride in it Nobbly-Knees, because you won't and anyway we're getting an even bigger one, we're getting a STRETCH LIMONSY," Mona was able to bare her fangs at

Angela – as a serious warning.

Only Angela wasn't warned. During morning Show and Tell, she didn't show and tell at all. She showed off and boasted horribly.

First about her new talking watch.

Then about her singing hairband which sang *Walking Talking Baby Doll* and *Yankee Doodle* and there were only ten in the world and she had two of them.

And then, most horribly of all, she showed off about her new pair of purple trainers that tied their own laces when she pressed a matching remote control.

Of course, everyone – even Miss Gotto – was amazed and desperate to be allowed to try it for themselves. But Angela wasn't letting anyone near that lace-tying remote. No way.

"You'll wear out the battery," she snapped in her new selfish voice. "Get your own if you can afford it which you can't because they cost a very, very, very

WALKING TALKING YANK

lot."

So, on behalf of everyone, Mona bared her fangs again. And again.

And she went "RRRRRRAAAARGH!"

And she made one of her elasticated spiders dangle scarily down Angela's neck.

But even then Angela didn't get the warning.

She just screamed horribly and told.

"Miss Gotto! Mona's being mean to me! Mona's making me creep. Mona's being a vampire again and you said no vampires in our classroom!"

This left Miss Gotto with no choice but to make Mona put her fangs, cloak and spiders in the lock-up cupboard till going-home time. Angela the More Horrible had won the first round against Mona the Vampire.

But Mona wasn't finished yet.

Chapter 3
A Flash of Inspiration

It was during a game of *Grandmother's Footsteps*. Mona was It and when she turned round she definitely saw Angela taking another step.

"Angela! Out!" she called.

"I wasn't moving!" yelled Angela.

"Yes you were!" yelled Mona.

"You were. I saw!" Lawrence, Charley-Knees' friend came over.

"Well, I'm not going out," said Angela as everyone crowded round. "And you can't make me. And anyway, watch this!"

And digging into her coat pocket she produced a small furry rabbit that wasn't a furry rabbit. It was a portable telephone and she was using it ...

Especially that Mona and I want to come home now. All right, I'll tell her we were going to ask her to Disneyland but now we're not and she can't ever come to our new house or swim in our pool or get to ride the real Starlight. OK. Goodbye!

YANKEE DOODLE!
WALKING TALKING
BABY DOLL

Mona paled with shock. Going to Disneyland and riding a *real* pony were two of the things she wanted to do most. Angela's horribleness had gone too far.

She put her hands on her hips.

"If you don't stop being so horrid and get back to being how you were when you were my best friend," she announced, "I'm going to ..."

"What?" scoffed Angela. "What are you going to do?"

For a second there was silence. Then, in the nick of time, Mona had the idea.

"Put the witches on you!"

"Oh yes? What witches?" Angela laughed.

"The ones I know," said Mona, growing more certain with each moment. "The ones I meet. On Wednesdays. In the churchyard. With their hubble-bubble cauldron to teach me their spells. The ones that give me and Fang rides on their broomsticks and are going to take us to Disneyland whenever we like."

Everyone stared at Mona, seeing the picture clearly. Excepting Angela.

"You're making it up, Mona Nashley. You're always making things up."

"I am not!" Mona retorted.

"All right then," Angela sneered. "Show me these witches. Take me to them. Not one day. This very Wednesday."

Chapter 4
The Witch Hunt Begins

And where do you think you're going to find witches by Wednesday? Fang hissed when Mona got home and told him about her brilliant idea. *Witches don't pop-up that easily.*

"We'll find some," said Mona. "We have to."

And that will be even worse, Fang hissed. *They might mistake me for one of theirs and grab me. I say let's drop the whole thing. Tell Angela they all died suddenly ...*

"I can't," said Mona putting on the vampire things she'd got back from Miss Gotto and adding some tomato sauce for extra scariness. "Angela has to be shown and that's all."

They set off on Mona's bike, cloaks flying.

We'll start with the churchyard

Mona wasn't allowed to ride further than Columbus Drive without a grownup following. But saving Angela from this disaster, she decided, had to be an exception.

She pedalled hard down Magellan Street – baring her fangs so no one would recognise her – checked ten times for cars at the pedestrian crossing and pushed her bike and Fang across Old Street.

AAAAAGH!

It was a lot darker in the churchyard than she'd expected.

In fact, it was so dark it was purple-black. The usually-green trees were purple-black. The toppled gravestones in their overgrown grass were purple-black. A light in the church snapped off and the church went purple-black.

Fang arched his back.

Mona went "RRRRRAAAAAAGH!" to frighten off any ghosts or vampire-

snatchers who might think they were easy prey.

Then pushing her bike as quickly as she could, she went to work.

"Witches," she called softly, taking care to keep on the right side of the gravestones. "Though we're vampires we won't hurt you. We just need you for a bit on Wednesday with a cauldron and some broomsticks— "

And then, suddenly, there it was ...

… a towering monster, black cloak flapping, in her path. It was lifting her into the air. Its shark's fin of white hair and its rows of shining white teeth gleamed. Screaming and struggling she raised her fist to pummel it. And didn't have to. Fang had sprung – expertly – to her rescue.

Chapter 5
Mona Grounded

"I just don't know how to apologise or thank you enough for bringing her home, Reverend Gregory. But I can promise she won't be messing about in your churchyard again."

Mona stood sulkily by the kitchen door listening.

She was in for it now, she knew, and it felt very unfair. After all it wasn't her fault that in the purple-blackness of the churchyard she and Fang had mistaken the Reverend Gregory for a monster.

Her father finished saying goodbye and came into the kitchen. Now *his* face was purple-black.

Not, he explained, because she'd mistaken a priest for a monster or Fang had scratched him, but because she'd gone beyond Columbus Drive without a grown-up.

"I'm afraid," he said, "when your mother hears about this, you won't be allowed out at all."

"Oh, no!" Mona jumped up and down. "You can't do that. After Wednesday will be all right. But not now!"

Mona's father eyed her suspiciously.

"Why? What do you have to do between now and Wednesday?"

"Nothing," said Mona.

"I don't believe you," said her father.

And he didn't and he wouldn't.

He just went on interrogating Mona until finally, when he was tucking her in, she cracked.

"I've got to find witches," she admitted. "By Wednesday. To show Angela and make her my best friend again."

"Then you'll have to find them in the garden," said her father firmly ...

...because your mother and I are agreed. You're grounded – till Thursday.

Chapter 6
Garden Witches Are Harder To Find

So, in Wednesday morning break, Mona told Angela of the change of plan.

"We're meeting the witches in my garden. Not the churchyard, OK?"

Angela was deeply suspicious. "Witches in your garden? You expect me to believe that?"

"Well, why not?" said Charley-Knees. "A garden's not much different to a churchyard. It's got graves. Of hamsters and spiders and ants and things."

"Yeah, and there are loads of cobwebs in our garden shed," said Mona. "It's a cobweb forest in there. And we've got all the frogs witches could want in our pond."

For a moment, Angela looked just a tiny bit nervous. But she soon recovered.

"All right. I'll ask if I can stay the night. So you can't get out of this which is what you're trying to do."

"More like you are," said Mona, "especially when you hear what spell I'm going to get them to put on you."

"Ha, ha!" said Angela stalking off to offer someone a chance to try her lace-tyer only to snatch it back just as they said yes.

Mona, Lily, Charley-Knees, Lawrence and Alex – Angela's second best friend before she turned horrible – walked over to their huddling-together place by the art room.

What Spell are you going to get them to put on her?

What about the Give-Away-Everything-You've-Got-To-Me Spell?

And suddenly finding their ideas very funny, the four started rolling round, laughing hysterically. Mona, alone, remained serious. She could feel her temperature rising.

"It's all right for you," she burst out. "Because you don't actually have to get any witches in your garden. But I do. So if you don't mind can you just stop being so silly!"

Her friends froze. For the first time since the witch-thing blew up, doubt showed on their faces.

"You don't mean," said Charley-Knees, "that you might not get any. I mean if you haven't got any witches then . . ." His voice trailed away.

"Her Horribleness might . . ." Lily tried.

"Rule for ever!" Lawrence managed.

"Well?" said Alex desperately. "Well?"

Mona took a deep breath ...

...of course I've got witches.

"I've got loads of witches. It's just that they're all at the churchyard and I'm not allowed there to get them. And garden witches are much, *much* harder to find. That's all!"

And she stalked off to find Miss Gotto and tell her about her rising temperature, and try to get to lie down till going-home time.

Chapter 7
Through the Cobwebs

"I'll have to go to bed," Mona announced as soon as she did get home. "I'm sick. Miss Gotto says I'm not but I am. And look at Fang. He's sick too."

Mona's mother felt her forehead.

"You seem cool enough to me," she said, "but I'll get the thermometer."

"Perfectly normal," she said, when she'd taken Mona's temperature. "Probably just a bit over-excited about

Angela staying the night. I was so glad when her mother asked me."

Mona's father looked up from tea-making.

"Were you?" he said. "From what I've heard that whole family is behaving very oddly since they hit the jackpot. And do we really want a best friend-turned-horrible for the night?"

"Exactly," said Mona. "Especially if I'm getting chicken pox which I'm sure I am even without a temperature. Ring her mother now and say don't come over or she'll catch huge, scratchy spots."

"Nonsense," said Mona's mother reaching for a small bottle of Rescue Remedy ...

A little of this Mona, and you'll be right as rain.

Mona swallowed the wretched remedy and slunk off with Fang to sulk in the grey, witchless garden.

She stared into the pond *willing* a witch to pop up through its slimy surface. She looked up at the fir tree *willing* broomsticks to be sticking out like cloves. Then she wandered over to the garden shed and closed her eyes.

"I'm closing my eyes now and counting to ten. Then I'm going to open the door and inside this shed there are going to be witches. Lots of them. Ready, steady, *one-two-three-four-five-six-seven-eight-nine-ten!*"

She pushed the door. A sheet of cobwebs brushed her face. Slowly she opened her eyes and peered through them, her heart beating wildly. But it was no good. Wishing hadn't worked.

There were garden chairs, tools and a rusting barbecue. But not a single witch.

And now Angela had arrived.

She could hear her mother calling for her.

Chapter 8
Seeing The Light

"Bedtime," said Mona's mother as she came in to the sitting room where Mona, Fang and Angela were watching TV. Mona scowled up at her. The sooner they went to bed, the sooner Angela would start asking for a witch to come to the bedroom window on a broomstick and take them for a ride.

"Not yet," she whined. "First a game of *Giggly Winks*."

"I'll go to bed, Mrs Nashley, if you say so," said Angela, sucking up horribly.

I'll just ring mummy on my furry bunny and say goodnight

It took less than a second, as far as Mona was concerned, for them to be washed, pyjamaed and tucked up – Mona on the put-me-up and Angela in Mona's bed.

"And I'm sorry, no story tonight," her mother said switching out the light. "Your father's at a meeting and I'm exhausted."

Immediately she was gone, Angela sat up.

"OK, then. Get on with it. Call the witches with your special witch whistle like you said. Come on. Ha, ha! See, I knew it, I knew it all along. You're the biggest liar. There are no witches. And now you definitely can't come to Disneyland with us or ride Starlight, for being such a liar."

Mona leapt out of bed.

"You just won't believe me, will you?"

"Seeing is believing," said Angela ...

Mona snapped on the bedside lamp and dived under the bed for her vampire things.

"OK. As soon as Fang and me are vampires because that's the only way they know us."

The only way they won't mistake me for one of theirs, hissed Fang.

So Angela watched impatiently while they got ready.

Mona took as long as she could.

But finally, there was nothing more she could add to their vampireyness.

She picked up her witch whistle, slowly, and walked the longest way to the window.

"Go on," said Angela. "Open it. Start whistling."

"Hmmm," said Mona. "Maybe next Wednesday would be better. Because I can smell the spell they're making out there. It's the worst spell. It's a Slug Spell. And you don't want to be turned into a slug of all things, do you?"

Slug Spells are worst

It didn't work. Angela just walked over and threw the window open.

"I'm not afraid of spells. So whistle."

Mona sighed inwardly. There was no way out. Angela's horribleness was here to stay. She was about to throw down the witch whistle – actually a Christmas cracker whistle – and admit defeat.

And then ... she saw the light.

It was a flickering light. The light of tall candles, shining through the cobwebs on the shed windows.

And in the light Mona could clearly make out the shapes of three tall black hats – and three *very* hooked, *very* warty noses.

She wanted to whoop with happiness. But instead she spoke calmly.

"I only hope it isn't the Slug Spell they're making out there, Angela Because if it is you're *slime*. Look!"

Chapter 9
A Rather Nasty Stew

"Come on," whispered Mona creeping onto the landing. "It's easy. We just sneak downstairs, out of the dining room door, behind the hydrangeas and we'll see everything."

"Your mother will kill us!" Angela's whisper was wobbly.

"My mum wouldn't kill a pirhana fish."

"You go. I'll watch from the window."

"You're just afraid."

Of course she is, hissed Fang. *So am I.*

"I'll get them not to turn you into a slug."

"Not into ANYTHING," bargained Angela, trembling wildly.

Mona herself was trembling by the time they got to the hydrangeas.

Only she was trembling with wonder at just how amazingly things could turn out when you really needed them to.

The witches had now come out of the shed and placed a cauldron on the grass. They started singing and dancing round it. And every word they sang could be clearly heard from the shrubbery.

Oh hubble bubble, toil and trouble,
Add some eyebrows, warts and stubble.
Add some cockroach grubs and grime,
Jellied venom, slugs and slime.
And when we've made this brilliant brew,
We'll give a mug to those of you
Who turn against a once-best friend
In horrid ways that most offend,
And as you sip our gorgeous grog
You'll turn yourself - not to a frog,
But to the loving friend you were
So be our guest - come.... have a STIR!

Mona drew in her breath sharply. Three broomsticks were pointing straight at Angela. Excepting that Angela was no longer there. She was streaking back into the house like a bat from a belfry - Fang only a few paces behind her.

Chapter 10
Farewell Notes and a Bit of a Mystery

"Well, it worked!" Mona burst in from school the next day. "It was amazing. Angela was nice to everyone! *Even* Charley-Knees. Now the whole class wants to see the witches. And I said they could on this next Wednesday!"

"Now wait a minute," Mona's mother stepped in.

"Oh please! They'll all bring sleeping bags ...!"

"The answer is no and that's that. And besides, I'm very cross with you for telling everyone there were witches in our garden in the first place."

"But there were," said Mona starting to snivel.

Her father took her and Fang to the sofa for a cuddle-up.

"By the way," he said taking a letter out of his pocket. "I found this pinned to the garden shed today. Shall I read it?"

"Mmm," sniffed Mona.

So Mona's father opened the letter and read it out ...

Dear Mona the Vampire,

What a pleasure it was to catch a glimpse of you in the hydrangeas last night – together with your best friend and nearly fearless cat, Fang.

Unfortunately we have to go away now FOR EVER AND EVER. So we'll never be in your garden ever again – or even in your neighbourhood – EVER!

Farewell!

Yours

The Wednesday-Night Witches

"Oh well," Mona cheered up instantly. "That's all right then. I'll just show everyone the letter and they'll know why they can't come and see them."

Then she and Fang went outside to sniff around for witch-evidence.

"Bit of a mystery, about these witches," said Mona thoughtfully as they hunted. "I just remembered. They were wearing garden wellies like ... like my dad's."

Ah well, purred Fang, *does it matter? And anyway, with mysterious things, its always nice to be left with a bit of the mystery.*

Mona the Vampire
by Hiawyn Oram
Illustrated by Sonia Holleyman

Collect all the fangtastic *Mona the Vampire* stories!

☐ 1 **Mona the Vampire and the Hairy Hands**
ISBN 1 84121 859 6 £2.99

☐ 2 **Mona the Vampire and the Big Brown Bap Monster**
ISBN 1 84121 861 8 £2.99

☐ 3 **Mona the Vampire and the Tinned Poltergeist**
ISBN 1 84121 855 3 £2.99

☐ 4 **Mona the Vampire and the Jackpot Disaster**
ISBN 1 84121 857 X £2.99

Look out for the novelty book,

☐ **Mona the Vampire's Diary by Sonia Holleyman**
ISBN 1 86039 8804 £8.99

Mona the Vampire books are available from all good bookshops,
or can be ordered direct from the publisher:
Orchard Books, PO BOX 29, Douglas IM99 1BQ
Credit card orders please telephone 01624 836000
or to fax 01624 837033
or e-mail: bookshop@enterprise.net for details.

To order please quote title, author and ISBN
and your full name and address.
Cheques and postal orders should be
made payable to 'Bookpost plc'.
Postage and packing is FREE within the UK
(overseas customers should add £1.00 per book).

Prices and availability are subject to change.